LITTLE MALLORY'S GARDEN OF FRIENDS

By
Melinda McQueen

Copyright © 2025 by Melinda McQueen

All rights reserved.

Dedication:

This book is dedicated to
children who feel like they don't
Belong because they are different.
Please know that you have a purpose
And you're loved more than you know!

This book is also dedicated to
The children who go out of their way
To befriend others who feel left out.
You are shining stars!

LITTLE MALLORY'S GARDEN OF FRIENDS

MELINDA MCQUEEN

The day was bright
With few clouds in sight.

Little Mallory's first day of school
made her tummy turn into a butterfly's pool.

The other kids stared,
and only a few half-smiles of care.

LITTLE MALLORY'S GARDEN OF FRIENDS

Looking around, Little Mallory felt out of place,
for they all ran away.

Little Mallory followed them out to the playground,
wheeling herself out, her wheels went around
and around.

Watching the kids play,
Little Mallory sat alone, out of the way.

LITTLE MALLORY'S GARDEN OF FRIENDS

Seeing them pointing at her,
everything became a blur.

She wasn't surprised; she knew it would be like this,
Little Mallory had already experienced it, though
only six.

Then, a little girl came and stood by her side.
"What's your name? Mine is Sky!"
"I'm Mallory, thanks for coming to talk."
"You're welcome. I don't mind at all."

LITTLE MALLORY'S GARDEN OF FRIENDS

But just as she said so,
a few girls came to let her know...

"We're playing Hopscotch, Sky, come on!"
And again, Little Mallory was left alone.

Little Mallory couldn't join most games
that kids her age played.
This made her sad,
and feel all kinds of bad.

LITTLE MALLORY'S GARDEN OF FRIENDS

Try as she may to fit in,
she didn't have a friend.

As days went by,
Little Mallory could only sigh.
What she would give
to have just one friend.

LITTLE MALLORY'S GARDEN OF FRIENDS

One day, she saw a group of girls laughing,
who kept looking her way, giggles never lacking.

Little Mallory decided she was doomed to be alone,
so, she made up a game of her own.

LITTLE MALLORY'S GARDEN OF FRIENDS

MELINDA MCQUEEN

Letting her imagination take her far away,
she entered into her own little world of play.

Where there were many flowers
and a big, smiling sun
who warmed them all as one.
For all flowers were different colors and shapes,
and the big, smiling sun shone upon
each in their place.

LITTLE MALLORY'S GARDEN OF FRIENDS

MELINDA MCQUEEN

Little Mallory tended to the flowers of her garden
to help the big, smiling sun at its pardon.
Watering the flowers with kind words of encouragement,
for she knew how much kindness meant.

"Can I sit with you?" asked Sky at lunchtime
"Sure, that would be fine."

LITTLE MALLORY'S GARDEN OF FRIENDS

"What are you drawing?" Sky asked.
"My flower garden." Mallory said as she sat back.
"You have a flower garden at home?"
"Nope. This flower garden is my own."

"Where is it?"
"It's in my mind." Mallory insisted.
"You mean make-believe?"
"I guess that's what I mean."

LITTLE MALLORY'S GARDEN OF FRIENDS

MELINDA MCQUEEN

"Your drawing is pretty."
"Thanks. I'm trying to capture what I see."

"Do you have more drawings in
that notebook?"
"Yes, but you can't look."
"Why not? Can't I have a peek?"
"Sorry, but I don't let just anyone see."

LITTLE MALLORY'S GARDEN OF FRIENDS

"Not even your friends??"
"I don't have any, except for the friends
in my garden…"
"We're friends, aren't we??"
Little Mallory was surprised, "You want to be friends
with me??"

"Of course I do!"
"Thanks, I'd like that, too."

Little Mallory smiled and passed the notebook,
and instantly, a friendship took.

LITTLE MALLORY'S GARDEN OF FRIENDS

"These drawings are great!"
"Thanks! It's my make-believe world!" Mallory exclaimed.
"Tell me more about this flower garden of yours."
Sky's smile was pure.

"It's a place where everyone is different in their way,
and yet they're the same.
They accept each other for who they are,
reminding one another of their own special art."

"Why did you create it?"
Little Mallory's eyes unlit,
"I can't play most games other kids play,
and I feel left out and far away."

LITTLE MALLORY'S GARDEN OF FRIENDS

"Oh," sighed Sky, "that must be sad,
it must make you feel bad."
"It makes me feel lonely,
because kids don't know how to include me."

"Well, I'm your friend,
friends to the end!"

Little Mallory was happy to have a friend,
someone in whom she could depend.

LITTLE MALLORY'S GARDEN OF FRIENDS

Days went by and the kids ignored her still.
Little Mallory was hurt by their ill will,
but she was grateful to have a friend in Sky,
who was almost always by her side.

"What are you drawing today?"
"A sun with a smiley face!"
"I thought you only drew flowers."
"Flowers need the sun's power."

"Oh, I see. You're drawing the sun for your garden!"
"Yep, the flowers need rechargin'!"
Little Mallory giggled; she enjoyed sharing
with someone—
to finally have a friend to share her garden was fun.

LITTLE MALLORY'S GARDEN OF FRIENDS

The other kids continued to shy away,
busy in their time of play.
What she wouldn't give to participate
in their childhood games.

One day during Recess, Little Mallory came
out to find
a group of kids surrounding Sky.
Once they spotted her, they giggled as they looked
her way,
and her smile began to fade.

Then, all at once, they came over to her,
surrounding Mallory, faces became a blur.
Smiles and laughter everywhere
as Sky took control of Little Mallory's chair.

LITTLE MALLORY'S GARDEN OF FRIENDS

MELINDA MCQUEEN

"Where are we going?" Mallory's cocked an eye.
"I'm not telling! It's a surprise!"

Little Mallory laughed in delight
as Sky gave her a bumpy ride.
Soon, they were at the site
and Mallory couldn't believe her eyes.

She saw flowers of every kind.
Everywhere she looked, many colors did she find.
Some were tall, some were just sprouting up,
but all were nourished by the sun above.

LITTLE MALLORY'S GARDEN OF FRIENDS

"This is beautiful!" Mallory beamed,
"They are the same flowers in my drawings… how can this be?"
"Well, I was inspired and asked the teacher for a garden." Sky replied,
"She thought it would be a good idea to try!"

"We all have been working together to bring your garden to life!"
"But why would you all do that?" Little Mallory asked, teary-eyed.
"Because you've taught us that,
like these flowers, we are all different, yet we're all the same!" said Matt.

LITTLE MALLORY'S GARDEN OF FRIENDS

"We want to be your friends and enjoy your garden
with you!"
"Really? I want to be friends with all of you, too!"
Looking around, she saw her peers nodding
in one accord,
Little Mallory smiled as her heart soared.

And there they were... tall, short, blonde, brunette,
Black, brown, and white, shy and outgoing, all were
jubilant.
Enjoying each other for who they were
and played as one,
As they blossomed beneath the great big sun.

Have you helped someone feel included?
If so, how did you?

Has someone included you? If so, how did it make you feel?

_____
_____
_____
_____
_____
_____
_____
_____
_____
_____
_____
_____

ABOUT THE AUTHOR

I live in East Texas with my husband, Andy. I love attending church and having a church family. I love going to the movies and spending time with Andy. I also spend time writing, of course. I am in a wheelchair with Cerebral Palsy, and I have so many people who take care of me, including my mother-in-law. I am blessed.

Other books by Melinda McQueen

Her Happiest Place (Novel)
Room Enough to Bloom (Children's Book)
Worshipping Thee in Poetry
A Trail of Words (Novel)
Finding a Home in Shear Forgiveness (Novel)
Rhyme Me a Life (Poetry)
Our Perfectly Timed Love (My true love story)

www.ingramcontent.com/pod-product-compliance
Lightning Source LLC
LaVergne TN
LVHW051036070526
838201LV00009B/219